Not sure how you passed all those chemythstry quizzes. Humph. I hope to see some more hextra credit spinning straw into gold out of you next year.

— Professor Rumpelstiltskin

FAIREST MAIDEN,
YOUR DAMSEL-IN-DISTRESSING DURING OUR HERO-IN-TRAINING CLASS WAS SIMPLY ENCHANTING. PLEASE ACCEPT MY SINCERE WISH FOR A FAIREST SUMMER. THOUGH THE SUN'S RAYS WILL CEASE TO BE AS BRIGHT WITHOUT YOUR PRESENCE, I LOOK FORWARD TO ONCE AGAIN SHARING YOUR WONDROUS COMPANY NEXT YEAR.

— HOPPER CROAKINGTON II
(Ribbet!)

What an enchanting year! I know there were a few fairy fails, but hey, us royals are destined to face a few challenges every spell and again, right? I'll always remember our silly hext messaging during Damsel-in-Distressing and the off-the-book time we all had at Thronecoming. Charm you later!

— Apple White

Your Crownculus was fairy impressive this year. Now, if only you would stop hexting during class, you'd be on your way to a royal destiny. Enjoy your summer.

— Her Majesty, the White Queen

It sure was a hexciting year, wasn't it? Thanks for sticking by me when I, you know, went off-script in a major way. You're a true friend 'till the end. Here's to next year and writing our own destinies. It's going to be legendary!

— Raven Queen

Of course I will grace your yearbook with my signature. I'm sure you're honored.

Daring *Charming*

REMEMBER TO ALWAYS FOLLOW YOUR ROYAL DESTINY. UPHOLDING YOUR FAIRYTALE STORY IS OF THE UTMOST IMPORTANCE.
— HEADMASTER GRIMM

STAY ON! LIVE ON! WONDERLANDIFUL! STORYBOOK FRIENDSHIP WILL ALWAYS BE — AROUND THE CLOCK AND MOONBEAMS GONE OUT HANDS TOGETHER AGAIN AS THESE! SUMMER ENCHANTING AND HAPPILY SUN DAFFODILS BEES — MEADOWS, CREAM LETTER — MADDIE

Have a hexcellent summer. Never stop smiling.
~Kitty Cheshire
=^..^=

Ever After High™

YEARBOOK

A Hexciting Year at Ever After High

Scholastic Inc.

Artwork ©: Dreamstime: cover center flowers (Alexandra Shkarupa), cover side cartouche (Vadym Nechyporenko), cover frames (Verdateo), 51–52, 76–77 fabric background (Kmiragaya), 78–83 frame, 88 frame (Ela Kwasniewski), 88–89 border (Kjolak), 90 frame (Extezy), 91 frame (Designrepository), 92 frame (100ker), 93 frame (Francesco Abrignani); Fotolia: cover corner cartouche, 3 frame (setory), 9 frame (Tatiana Prihnenko); iStockphoto: 35 rolling pin (KeithBishop), 92 ring watermark (kristina-s), 93 cupcake (ma_rish); Thinkstock/KsushaArt: 23 seashell background.

ISBN 978-0-545-72368-8

10 9 8 7 6 5 4 3 2   14 15 16 17 18 19/0
Written by Rebecca Paley
Printed in the U.S.A.
First printing, September 2014

40

TABLE OF CONTENTS

Welcome to Ever After High

Where the End is Just the Beginning . . .

LEGACY-YEARS SETTLE IN: Students snap mirror-selfies and chat on their way to class.

Dear Students,

It is my pleasure to serve as headmaster at Ever After High School, which since its founding many stories ago (by *me*) has been dedicated to instructing, enlightening, and inspiring new generations of fairy-tale heirs. Our mission is to preserve the stories that have guided Ever After toward happiness and prosperity for ages.

Sometimes this is not an easy task. But always remember that following in the fabled footsteps of your parents is a responsibility of the highest order. Upholding the stories handed down to us is not just done out of tradition, but for the protection of all our Ever Afters. Without these stories—our stories—Ever After would cease to exist.

And so, at the core of our school is not parties or romances or unroyal-like shenanigans, but rather the fulfillment of our destinies and all fairytale destinies to come. As headmaster of this most legendary institution, I am certain that you will all embrace this privileged responsibility and will do your fairy best to ensure Ever After remains a place where storybook endings always come true.

Congratulations to all the legends of tomorrow!

Yours forever after,

Milton Grimm

Ever After High Campus

EVER AFTER HIGH
CASTLETERIA

EVER AFTER HIGH
GRIMMNASIUM

A APPLE AND RAVEN'S ROOM

B DORMS

C CASTLETERIA

D BALCONY

E GRIMMNASIUM

F DESTINY COURT

G SPORTS FIELD

H BRIDGE TO BOOK END

I BRIDGE TO CONCERT HALL

J LIBRARY

Letter from the Editor

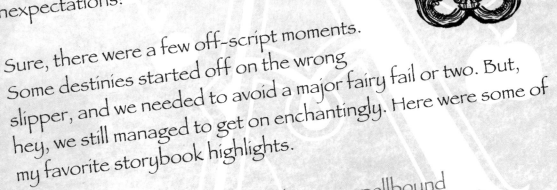

Hello, fairest fellow students! Apple White, your royal yearbook editor-in-chief here. It has been a spelltacular year at Ever After High. And I think we can all agree that it has totally surpassed everyone's hexpectations!

Sure, there were a few off-script moments. Some destinies started off on the wrong slipper, and we needed to avoid a major fairy fail or two. But, hey, we still managed to get on enchantingly. Here were some of my favorite storybook highlights.

Blondie Lockes kept us spellbound with her MirrorCast "Just Right!"

Briar Beauty's study parties were more than just page-rippers. They had us acing Professor Rumpelstiltskin's wicked-hard tests!

A royal shout-out to Cupid for reviving the spellebration True Hearts Day.

And who will ever forget when Cedar Wood turned her hair green by washing it with troll tears? Oh my godmother!

What a royal nightmare that was!
— Cedar

But I'm sure everyone has their favorite fairytale moments, and our charmtastic team of yearbook mirror-photographers managed to capture them all! So enjoy this year's hexquisite yearbook. After all, we only live once upon a time!

Royally yours,

Apple White

Apple White

Spellbinding Student Life

Ever After High bustles with a cauldron-load of activity at the beginning of the school year. From dorm-room decorating choices and book-to-school parties to new class schedules and games of pixie football, there's always spelltastic fun brewing!

Ever After High

Legacy-Year Students
Settle In

Legacy Year is one of the most hexciting times for students at Ever After High. This is the year they declare their fairytale destiny and sign the Storybook of Legends! But in between classes and Legacy Day rehearsal, students take a spell to catch up in the halls.

BEST FRIENDS 'TILL THE END: Legacy-year students Apple White, Briar Beauty, and Blondie Lockes snap a quick mirror-selfie before dashing off to Throne Room.

UGH, I CAN'T BELIEVE THEY PUT THIS AWKWARD MIRROR-SNAPSHOT OF ME IN HERE. GUESS I'LL NEVER BE AS CHARMING AS MY BROTHER.
DEX

CHARMED, I'M SURE: Dexter Charming, son of King Charming, chats with Raven Queen, daughter of the Evil Queen. It's not often royals and rebels mingle. But this year, all the rules seem to be off-the-book.

Damsels in Debate

For the first time in forever after, Apple White ran *opposed* in the Royal Student Council Elections by Madeline Hatter. The girls worked their crowns off in the Charmitorium debate, but the school remained divided. Luckily, they came up with an enchanting idea to be co-presidents. Sometimes going off-script can have a happy ending.

Maddie debates against Apple . . . speaking in Riddlish. We're not quite sure what she said, but it sounded tea-rrific!

Hats over crowns forever!
— Raven

Apple outlines her plans for Royal Dances, Royal Fundraisers, and Royal Canned Food Drives.

Dorms Fit for
Royals (and Rebels!)

The dorm rooms at Ever After High reflect each student's personality. Legacy-year students enjoy adding charming touches to make their rooms unique. It's a spella-good time letting their true destinies shine!

PRINCESS PERFECT: Apple White's dorm room décor is truly the fairest of them all!

SEEING PURPLE: Apple wanted to help her roommate, Raven, feel right at home. So she stuck to the script and redecorated her roomie's side to look perfect for an Evil Queen!

TEA-RRIFIC!: Madeline Hatter's style sense is straight out of Wonderland. Her dorm décor proves there's always a spot for a spot of tea—even on top of the chandelier!

STEALING OUR HEARTS: From throne sitting rooms to treelined hallways, the boys' dormitories are just right for the future Prince Charmings and Brave Huntsmen of Ever After High.

Castleteria Mishaps

*Oh my godmother!
I will never forget that
day. It was the biggest
mess since Legacy Day!*
—Apple

Even if destiny is written in stone, that doesn't mean things at Ever After High can't go a little Wonderlandian-cuckoo every now and again. Like the time Raven Queen went completely off-script by *not* signing the Storybook of Legends. That led to a wicked-messy food fight in the Castleteria! Has everyone flipped their crown?

A WICKED MESS: The Castleteria was the site of an ogre-sized FOOD FIGHT! Mis-devious Kitty Cheshire was behind the gastronomical battle . . .

. . . but all the students seemed willing to throw their share of fairy fries, spellghetti, and pizza. Good thing the Castleteria wasn't serving its legendary stone soup that day!

Fairytale Festivals

Every year, festivals are held in honor of each royal's legend.
Students love spellebrating along with their favorite fairytale friends!

Beauty Sleep Festival

This year's Beauty Sleep Festival, in honor of Briar Beauty,
was particularly restorative. Special props to Ashlynn Ella
for bringing the shipment of fuzzy slippers from the Glass
Slipper shoe boutique. They were fairy comfy!

"Totally enchanting!"

–Briar Beauty

Apple Festival

As co-president of the student council, Apple
attends every festival. But the Apple Festival
holds a special place in her heart. Students
were relieved that not a single turnover,
piece of bread, or slice of pie was poisoned.
And the whole school smelled enchantingly
of cinnamon and nutmeg for days!

You're Invited to
The Apple Festival

Please join us for

The Little Mermaid Festival

Little Mermaid Festival

Everyone flipped their tails for this year's Little Mermaid Festival down at Looking Glass Beach. Cerise and Daring set up an intense game of beach volleyball that ended with everyone cooling off in the ocean. And the evening's clam dig was a swimming success!

Spring Cleaning Festival

Only a school as charming as Ever After High could make scrubbing cauldrons and floors a party. The Spring Cleaning Festival in honor of Ashlynn Ella had royals and rebels alike removing old spell stains, vacuuming trails of bread crumbs, and sweeping up pixie dust. But it ended with a grand ball, which had everyone rocking well past midnight.

"We have to be royally responsible for the enchanting world we live in."
—Ashlynn Ella

Academics

Academics at Ever After High never let up. Students can always be found hitting the spellbooks, firing up the cauldrons, twirling their wands, opening up magic bags, bottling up bubbling brews . . . well, you get it. Ruling a kingdom (or ruining it—if that's your destiny) takes a hexaustive amount of training!

Fairy Favorite Classes

Class schedules are handed out by the Fairy-Godmothers-in-Training and are perfectly suited to each student's royal or wicked destiny.

CLASS SCHEDULE

Kingdom Management

Cooking Class-ic

Crownculus

Damsel-In-Distressing

Princessology 101

Heronomics

Castle Design

CLASS SCHEDULE

General Villainy

Home Evilnomics

Poison Fruit Theory

History of Evil Spells

Kingdom Mis-management

Witchness Management 101

Beast Training & Care

Students sound off on their favorite classes at Ever After High!

"*Dance Class. I am part swan, after all.*" —*Duchess Swan*

"ADVANCED WOOING. I need all the practice I can get so I don't turn into a frog every time I see a princess!" —Hopper Croakington II

"Muse-ic class. What, you thought only princesses could sing power ballads?" —RAVEN QUEEN

"HERO TRAINING. IT'S TAUGHT BY MY DAD, SO IT KIND OF RUNS IN THE FAMILY." —DEXTER CHARMING

"CHEMYTHSTRY. I'M TEA-RRIFIC AT POTIONS!" —MADELINE HATTER

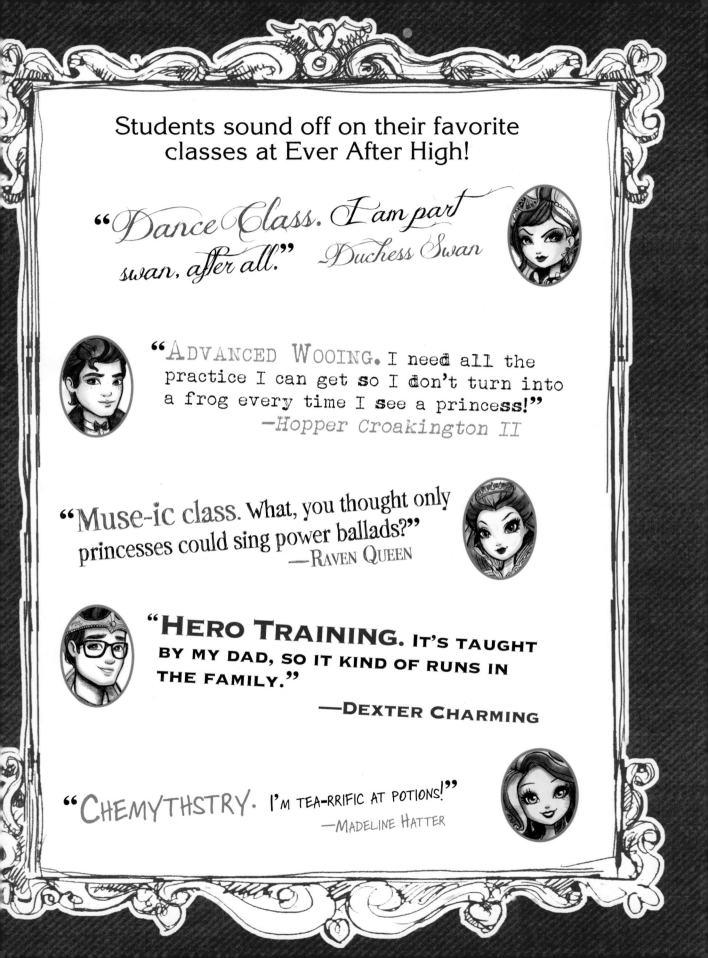

Hitting the Spellbooks

Science & Sorcery

Professor Rumpelstiltskin is infamous for giving tests where grades across the board are "Fairy Fail"! Why? Because he wants his students to ask for hextra credit, which they can only earn by spinning straw into gold!

Daring! How did you know I'd be here?

Catching Damsel in Distress is kind of my thing.

Damsel-in-Distressing

During one class of Damsel-in-Distressing, the princes got caught up in a separate rescue mission for Heroics 101, so the princesses had to figure out a way to rescue themselves. Now that was quite the lesson!

Daring Charming is so good at rescuing damsels in distress, even he doesn't know when he's going to run into them!

$$\frac{ty}{tx} + P(x)t = Q(x)$$

Solve for "x" where "P" is the number of princesses in class, "Q" is the number of future queens, and "t" is the number of toads who need kisses to turn into princes.

Crownculus

Taught by Her Majesty, the White Queen, this class is just as impossible as the six impossible things the teacher asks her students to imagine before class starts.

Home Evilnomics

Home Evilnomics is usually reserved for fairytale villains. But with all the royal and rebel rebellion going on this year, you never know who you're going to catch flipping the script!

Apple got more than she bargained for when she took Home Evilnomics to spite Raven. Her first assignment was to turn a sweet little bunny evil. Can you imagine anything so disenchanting?

Beast Training & Care

Not all classes take place within the castle walls. Each fall Professor Poppa Bear guides the legacy-year students into the Enchanted Forest to meet their woodland companions. These pets are drawn to their owners to help them on the quest toward destiny.

Cerise was especially enchanted to meet her direwolf pup, Carmine.

Not all students are assigned woodland companions. Kitty's pet caterpillar, Carroloo, came with her from Wonderland. And he's just as mischievous as she is!

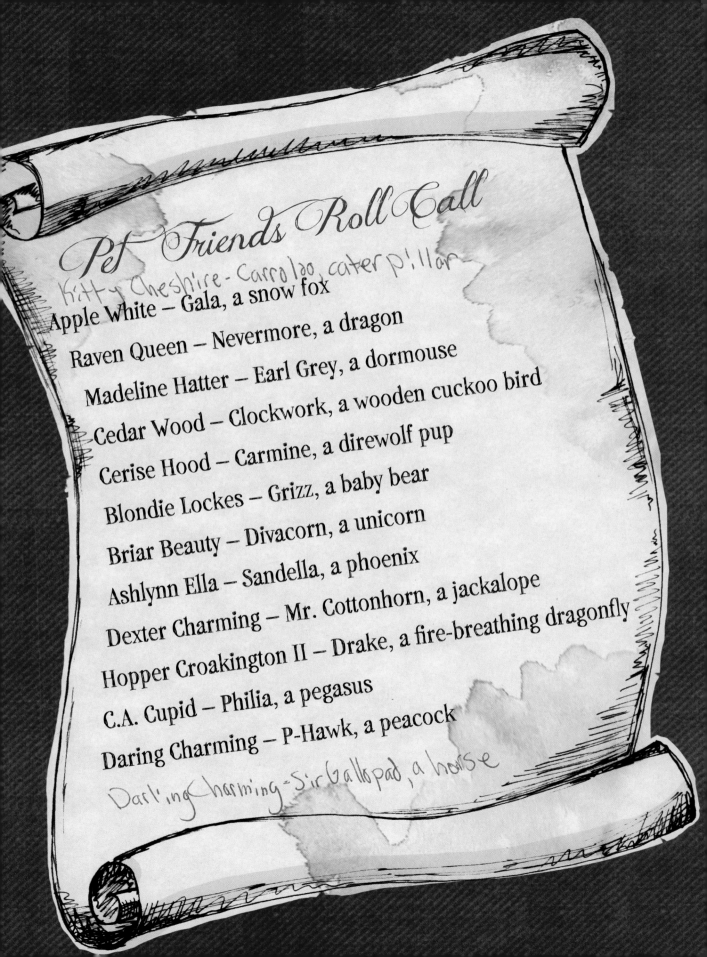

Pet Friends Roll Call

Kitty Cheshire – Carrolon, caterpillar

Apple White – Gala, a snow fox

Raven Queen – Nevermore, a dragon

Madeline Hatter – Earl Grey, a dormouse

Cedar Wood – Clockwork, a wooden cuckoo bird

Cerise Hood – Carmine, a direwolf pup

Blondie Lockes – Grizz, a baby bear

Briar Beauty – Divacorn, a unicorn

Ashlynn Ella – Sandella, a phoenix

Dexter Charming – Mr. Cottonhorn, a jackalope

Hopper Croakington II – Drake, a fire-breathing dragonfly

C.A. Cupid – Philia, a pegasus

Daring Charming – P-Hawk, a peacock

Darling Charming – Sir Gallopad, a horse

Grimmnastics

From applebatics and bookball to the
ever-popular decastleon, Ever After High
students give 'em hex out on the field.
It must be because we're charmed full of
school spirit! When you're running
full-speed toward destiny, you never
know when you'll need tower climbing or
beanstalk jumping skills in your basket.
Luckily, Coach Gingerbreadman and
the Ever After High Grimmnastics
teachers keep us on track.

On Track (Toward Destiny!)

Students warm up for laps on the Ever After High track.

Run, run, as fast as you can! So says Coach Gingerbreadman. The quick-bread leader of Grimmnastics makes sure students are fast on their toes. But it's just because he wants them to be ready in case some crazy old baker ever tries to eat them. So take a loaf off, Coach Gingerbreadman. You've trained us well.

This little piggy runs as fast as a huff and a puff!

I'll bet he was running from Cerise. Isn't it Wonderlandian weird how they're scared of her?
~ Kitty =^..^=

Don't worry, Coach. We'll never let them catch us!

A Word From Our Coach . . .

I keep things piping-hot in the Grimmnasium with routine basketball games. For all you commoners, that's when students carry baskets of treats while being chased by wolves. Nothing like a life-threatening chase to make those kids run, run as fast as they can. He-he. Everyone, that is, except Cerise. She seems to have a way with wolves and runs almost as fast as they do. I'm not sure what it is, but that girl creeps the breadcrumbs out of me . . .

Slaying the Odds

Dragon Slaying

Daring Charming continued to spellbind us with his magnificent Dragon Slaying skills. The one thing stronger than his heroic feats may just be his dazzling smile. It melts hearts faster than dragon fire.

Daring flashes us his trademark smile and wink . . .

. . . before facing off against his fiery foe!

Isn't he just so...daring!
—Apple

GRIMMNASTICS STARS

Croquet Team Captain

LIZZIE HEARTS

Archery Team Captain

HUNTER HUNTSMAN

Most Surprising
Grimmnastics Star

DEXTER CHARMING
*Behind his glasses and bumbling
manner, Dexter's really got game!*

Cross-Country Running

CERISE HOOD

Charm-Team Captain

APPLE WHITE

Royal Events

All work and no fun makes for an incredibly dull fairytale. So Ever After High's time-honored ceremonies are not only important but are also valid excuses (even in Headmaster Grimm's book) for having a ball! Plus, it means everyone has a reason to head down to the Village Mall for new gowns. There's nothing to get a party started like stylin' siren finery!

Briar's Book-to-School Party kicked off the school year to a page-ripping start with tunes pumped up by DJ En-Chant.

Students cheer as their fellow classmates declare their destinies on Legacy Day.

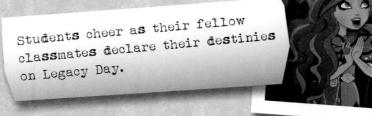

Legacy Day

Students prepare hexcitedly for Legacy Day. They had no idea what a page-turner it would be . . .

Legacy Day is the spellebration where students pledge to follow in the fabled footsteps of their parents—really the whole point of Ever After High. But Raven Queen pulled one whopper of a plot twist when she slammed the Storybook of Legends shut and declared she would write her own destiny! Because of her, Headmaster Grimm cancelled Legacy Day and the ball that follows it. Now, no one knows what will happen to their storybook destinies.

Best Quote of the Year (According to the Rebels)
"I am going to write my own destiny.
My happily ever after starts now!" –Raven

Worst Quote of the Year (According to the Royals)
"I am going to write my own destiny.
My happily ever after starts now!" –Raven

Apple White **signs** the Storybook of Legends while her royal friends look on.

Raven's friends watch nervously, just before she jumped script and slammed the Storybook of Legends shut! Oh, curses!

True Hearts Day

Though it's a little off-script (sorry, Headmaster!), Cupid couldn't help herself when she learned about the long-lost festival of "True Hearts Day." This fabled spellebration encourages everyone to follow their true-heart's desire. Naturally, Briar Beauty was all over the idea of an off-the-book party. So she helped Cupid plan a page-ripper of a dance complete with True-Hearts tunes by DJ Melody Piper!

Headmaster Grimm suspected something was up. And Duchess Swan didn't help with her sneaky tattling. Luckily, Hopper Croakington II came to the rescue with an eloquent excuse, even if he was in frog form.

SPELL WHAT?!: Ashlynn Ella and Hunter Huntsman dropped a bombspell on everyone by announcing that they're an item. A royal and a rebel dating? What a plot twist!

PUMP IT UP: Students danced on the floor 'till midnight with the rockin' tunes by none other than the Pied Piper's daughter, Melody Piper!

TRUE-LOVE TRIANGLE: Raven received a love letter from "D. Charming" and mistakenly thought it was from Daring! Meanwhile, Dexter has a royal crush on Raven, but is oblivious to Cupid's crush on him. Come on, people. True love shouldn't be this hard!

THRONECOMING

How enchanting was that night! I've never had so much fun getting fairest! ~Cupid

Thronecoming came and went this year—without a Thronecoming King and Queen being crowned! Dex and Melody Piper did a spelltacular job being in charge of the voting. But when the MirrorNet voting system went down, we never got to know who the lucky couple was. Oh, well, it's no secret Apple wins pretty much every year. But this wasn't any ordinary year for the festival. So we, the yearbook committee, came up with our own winners!

Fairest of the Ballroom

Apple White

utest from Crown to Toe

Blondie Lockes

Most Stylin' Siren

C.A. Cupid

Off-Campus Magic: The Village of Book End

When the students of Ever After High need a break from hitting the spellbooks, they head straight to the Village of Book End. There's no better place to hang out and maybe shop for a new fairest ball gown or two. The Hocus Latte Café keeps us going through those late-night cram sessions with wicked hot-chocolate. And the Beanstalk Bakery is the favorite hot-spot for an after-ball snack.

Apple and Briar visit with Ashlynn at the Glass Slipper shoe boutique.

Students enjoy a sunny afternoon in the village shopping and hanging out.

Hocus Latte Café

The Hocus Latte Café, with its permanent aroma of chocolate, remains a favorite student hangout. But sometimes more than coffee is brewing at this village hotspot. The Hocus Latte Café is known to be the place where an off-book plot or two has started!

Ashlynn and Hunter (in disguise) meet up at the café to discuss their secret relationship. Oh my godmother!

We asked students how they like their hocus lattes. Here's what they had to say:

Apple White: "With extra nutmeg, of course!"

Hunter Huntsman: "Triple-mint with chocolate syrup."

Briar Beauty: "I like mine with a lotta, lotta, *lotta* cream."

OMGM...Love!
—Ashlynn

Glass Slipper Shoe Boutique

Ashlynn Ella works part time at the Glass Slipper, so she knows how to keep her best friends forever after looking stylish with the perfect shoes. From glass heels to fuzzy slippers, Ashlynn definitely has a sixth sense— shoe sense!

Mad Hatter of Wonderland's Hat and Tea Shoppe

...eapots rattle and whistle on every table of this ...psy-turvy tea shop. Booths are forever crowded ...ll of students drinking wonderlandiful concoctions ...ch as Milkflower Brew or Spritzle-Fizzle Tea. It's ... little cramped, but in our book, it's the perfect cozy ...ook for a spot of tea!

Spellacular Students

Royal, rebel, wicked, or just plain nice—one thing you would never say about the students of Ever After High is that we are boring. You will not find that word in our storybook! Our student body is diverse in opinion, magical powers, even species, which means we don't always get along. There have been times when people get a little huffy and puffy. But we always close the chapter on that book and move on to happier plots. Simply put: From crown to toe, this is the best school ever!

Apple White

The Fairest One of the Halls

As the co-president of the Royal Student Council (and future queen), Apple is one of the fairest, most popular, and all-around nicest people you'll ever meet. But beneath her charming looks, she's truly a heartfelt friend to the end.

VOTED MOST-LIKELY TO

Rule a future kingdom charmingly

ACTIVITIES

Co-president of the Royal Student Council; Editor of the Yearbook

Apple and her BFFA, Briar, walk to Throne Room.

Apple shined as always debating in the student-council elections.

Raven Queen

Royally REBELLIOUS

Raven threw Ever After High into a fairy-tailspin when she decided not to declare her destiny as the Evil Queen. Half the school was horrified—their happily ever afters were in jeopardy! But the other half thought she was a hero. Raven just wants to have a choice . . . is that so bad?

⚜ —VOTED MOST-LIKELY TO— ⚜
Go off-book

⚜ —ACTIVITIES— ⚜
Reading adventure novels; music; baby-sitting for her family cook's little boys when she's back home (Does that sound like someone who is evil?)

Best friend 'till "the end," Madeline Hatter, helps Raven settle in.

Raven lends an ear when Cerise Hood has a problem.

Briar Beauty

Life's a Dream

Destined to sleep for one hundred years in her fairytale legend, Briar Beauty is Ever After High's go-to royal for planning off-the-book parties. As Briar likes to say, "If I'm going to sleep for one hundred years, I've gotta live it up now!"

❖— SECRET TALENT —❖

Super hearing for gossip, but only while she's asleep

❖— ACTIVITIES —❖

Party Planner-in-Chief of the Royal Student Council; Hextreme Sports

Briar, Cupid, and Hopper Croakington II secretly plan the True Hearts Day dance.

Our favorite sleeping beauty, catching some pre-Throne Room zzz's.

Madeline Hatter

Mischief and MADNESS

Madeline Hatter is one of the few students who made it out of Wonderland before it was poisoned by the Evil Queen's wicked magic. Even still, Maddie is BFFAs with Raven, the Evil Queen's daughter. It just goes to show that Maddie's heart is as big as a bottomless teapot!

⚜ KNOWN FOR ⚜

Speaking Riddlish. That's a language of rhymes and riddles, usually only spoken in Wonderland.

⚜ ACTIVITIES ⚜

Co-president of the Royal Student Council; Wonderland Tea Party Committee Chair

Giles Grimm, Headmaster Grimm's secret brother, is cursed by a Babble Spell to speak Riddlish. Maddie can understand him . . . sort of.

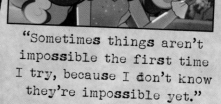

"Sometimes things aren't impossible the first time I try, because I don't know they're impossible yet."

Ashlynn Ella

You Only Live Once Upon a Time

As the daughter of Cinderella, Ashlynn is kind, compassionate, and adores all wildlife. She's also obsessed with shoes. Whenever she sees a pair she simply has to have them. It's no wonder she works part time at the Glass Slipper shoe boutique.

❖ WHAT OTHERS ADMIRE ABOUT HER ❖
She doesn't take anything for granted, even royalty

❖ ACTIVITIES ❖
Environmental Magic Club; Sales Associate at the Glass Slipper

Ashlynn's one weakness is shoes. She can't control herself around them.

Ashlynn gives her not-so-secret boyfriend Hunter a heart flower on True Hearts Day.

Hunter Huntsman

Destined to become the brave huntsman in any number of storybook legends, it's unusual for Hunter to be dating Ashlynn. After all, she's fated to marry a prince. But being the brave huntsman he is, we know Hunter isn't going to let anything stand in his way.

❖ KNOWN FOR ❖

Ripping off his shirt while an invisible trio of trumpets blast whenever a damsel is in distress. It's just something that happens around huntsmen.

❖ ACTIVITIES ❖

Hunting—but not to kill. The thought of hurting an animal makes him faint.

A handcrafted picnic table is just the right way to surprise your forever-after sweetheart.

Hunter faces off against Pesky, a rambunctious little squirrel.

Cerise Hood

CLOAKED in Mystery

Cerise is one of the most mysterious girls at school. She's never seen without her hood pulled down low over her head. But during this year's Thronecoming bookball game, she really came out of the shadows and led the EAH team to victory. Spelltacular!

⊰— WEIRD FACT —⊱

Pigs are afraid of her. No one knows why . . .

⊰— ACTIVITIES —⊱

Captain of the Cross-Country Team; eating meat

We wonder what Cerise and Raven are whispering about by the track?

There's always one student who gets caught in a photo with food in her mouth. Sorry, Cerise. It was storybook-bound to be you.

Cedar Wood

Wait a Splinter!

Cedar is one of the newest students at Ever After High. Her father, Pinocchio, only recently carved her from wood. But unlike her father, Cedar is cursed to always tell the truth. It can be hard never telling a lie . . . and it can lead to some awkward fairy-fail moments!

⊹ KNOWN FOR ⊹

Always telling the truth. She's doesn't really have a choice. She also loves to paint.

⊹ ACTIVITIES ⊹

Arts & Crafts; Honest Opinions Club

Professor Jack B. Nimble instructs Cedar how to stretch the truth without lying for a class assignment.

When Cedar discovered Ashlynn and Hunter's secret relationship, it looked like the secret was out. Oh, curses!

Blondie Lockes

Just Right

Blondie Lockes is Ever After High's resident Blocksmith. It's not really a talent—locked doors open automatically for her. She insists she's a royal—just look at her golden curls! But her lock-picking skills have us thinking she's more rebellious than she lets on.

MOST HEXCITING MOMENT

Unlocking the Children's Treasury of Fairytale Heirlooms for all the students to explore

ACTIVITIES

Daily MirrorCast "Just Right";
Debate Team Captain

"Any juicy details for my MirrorCast show? Just talk to the mirror!"

Blondie tries to prove that troll tears make great shampoo . . . on Cedar Wood!

C.A. Cupid

Love Always Finds a Way

Cupid has played "matchmaker" ever since she transferred to Ever After High. With everyone's destinies up in the air, her advice is in high demand! Cupid's daily MirrorCast offers the perfect guidance for staying on-script in matters of the heart.

SPECIAL TALENT
Solving fairytale love problems

ACTIVITIES
Matchmaking; Ancient History Club

Cupid's MirrorCast keeps students shooting straight for true love.

Cupid explains the history behind the long-forgotten spellebration of True Hearts Day.

Lizzie Hearts

RESHUFFLE the Deck

Lizzie is destined to be the Queen of Hearts. But unlike Raven, she is perfectly happy to stay on-script. She can usually be found wandering around school crying, "Off with your head!" Lizzie assures us that, in Wonderland, those words mean "please" and "thank you." We certainly hope so . . .

TRANSFERRED FROM
Wonderland High

ACTIVITIES
Croquet Team Captain; Grimmnastics

Things tend to get sliced and diced wherever Lizzie goes . . .

"Off with their buds!"

Dexter Charming

NEVER OVERLOOK THE OBVIOUS

Dexter's older brother is Daring Charming. It can be hard growing up in the shadow of the future king. Dexter doesn't know what fairytale he's destined to be the prince in. So, he can be found in the Hero Training room most of the time, practicing for whatever destiny holds in store.

ACTIVITIES
Hero Training; Muse-ic practice

NOT-SO-SECRET CRUSH
Raven Queen (Oh, for fairy's sake, it was practically announced on Cupid's MirrorCast!)

Dexter was happy to campaign for Madeline in the Royal Student Council race.

Hmmm . . . whose locker could Dexter be leaving a love note on? Oh, Dex, never stop charming.

Daring Charming

His smile is SOOO spell binding!
—Apple

Charmed I'm Sure

Good looking, athletic, blinding-white smile. Yes, Daring Charming has it all. He certainly captured the hearts of the female yearbook mirror-photogaphers. They couldn't keep from swooning around him. But somehow, not a single photo of Daring came out unflattering.

⚜— ACTIVITIES —⚜
Captain of the Dragon-Slaying Squad;
Tooth Fairy Academy Sponsor

⚜— FUTURE WIFE —⚜
Apple White

⚜— PRESENT GIRLFRIEND —⚜
NOT Apple

Thank you, Daring. We have seen the light. And it is your smile.

Just because he and Apple end up together in their storybook legend doesn't mean they're an item, okay?

Humphrey Dumpty

Humphrey may look nerdy, but behind those eggshell glasses, he's a wicked-hot rap artist! He can break out a storybook beat on the fly, and we were spellbound by his latest tune in honor of Apple White. Take a listen!

ACTIVITIES
Head of the Ever After High Tech Club

KNOWN FOR
Hacking the MirrorNet

True-Rap *(An Ode to Apple White)*

Yo, yo, her name is Apple, and I can't grapple
with how fine and kind, you'd hafta be blind,
yo, blinded by the shine of her mind.
Gotta post a sign sayin'
beware the glare of that fair hair.
Can't bear the care of her stare.
One glance and you're tranced,
pierced by her lance, made to dance
to the boon of the tune of the
girl with the skin of pearl and golden curl.
She's Apple, yo,
and this be Humphrey on flow
with mo' rhymes I can throw
'till the day she becomes Snow
'till the Happily Ever then
'till the chick 'comes a hen.
The. End.

Duchess Swan

Show Your True Feathers

Wings down, Duchess is the best dancer at school, especially ballet. It's kind of fable-fated when your mom is the Swan Princess. If only Duchess made friends as well as she danced. It's no secret around school that she's ruffled a few feathers, and not in a good way.

ACTIVITIES

Leader of Dance Class-ic; scheming in general

LIFE GOAL

A Happily Ever After (even if she has to take someone else's to get it)

When Duchess discovered that Ashlynn and Hunter were secretly dating, she couldn't wait to spell it out for everyone.

BIRDS OF A FEATHER: Duchess's partner-in-villainy is Sparrow Hood.

Kitty Cheshire

Don't Worry
JUST SMILE

Though she's always smiling, we can't help feeling it's because Kitty has a sneaky secret or two. Perhaps her pet caterpillar from Wonderland, Carrolloo, knows what she's smiling about. Kitty kept disappearing whenever we tried to get a quote from her, so we just smiled back and walked away.

— ACTIVITIES —
Geografairy Club (she likes to know the lay of the land)

— BEST FRIENDS FOREVER AFTER —
Lizzie Hearts

Kitty relaxes for a spell on a branch outside her dorm room door.

Something tells us Kitty is up to a cauldron-load of mischief.

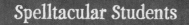

Holly O'Hair

Letting Her Hair Down

Holly's mom runs Rapunzel's Tower Hair Salon in the Village of Book End, so it's no wonder her hexquisite tresses always look as radiant as spun gold. Holly is destined to be the next Rapunzel and can usually be found practicing Damsel-in-Distressing in the towers on the Ever After High sports field.

⚜ ACTIVITIES ⚜
Damsel-In-Distressing; Writing fanfiction based on her friends' lives

⚜ HOLLY'S BEAUTY SECRET ⚜
Hair extensions and gallons of fairy-hair-care product!

⚜ HOLLY SAYS ⚜
"An active imagination is every princess's friend."

Poppy O'Hair

Think
OUTSIDE
THE TOWER

Poppy O'Hair is Holly's twin sister. However, she doesn't have a fairytale legend, so she's kind of an anomaly at Ever After High. She's freer than the pre-destined storybook heirs, and she puts all that extra energy into her heart's true passion—hair styling!

⚜ ACTIVITIES ⚜
Hair stylist

⚜ TRADEMARK LOOK ⚜
Short pixie-style haircut. She has to trim it every morning, because it grows so quickly.

⚜ STORYBOOK SECRET ⚜
Poppy is actually the first-born daughter of Rapunzel, but Holly is keeping her secret so Poppy can stay legacy-free!

Hopper Croakington I

LEAPING FOR LOVE

Hopper is one of the most eloquent princes at school. If only he could say what he feels when he's not a frog! Poor Hopper turns into a frog every time he gets tongue-tied around a beautiful princess. It tends to happen more often than not around a certain stylish yet sleepy royal.

⟡ ACTIVITIES ⟡
Advanced Wooing; Long Jump and Swim Team Captain

⟡ SECRETLY CRUSHING ON ⟡
A serious social butterfly

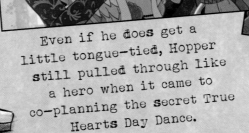

Even if he does get a little tongue-tied, Hopper still pulled through like a hero when it came to co-planning the secret True Hearts Day Dance.

"If only I possessed my poetic skills while in human form!"

Sparrow Hood

ROB from the RICH and GIVE TO ME!

Sparrow is the most rockin' rebel at Ever After High. If you were to ask him, he'd probably tell you he's a royal. (That's what he told us.) But with the bad boy, hexed-out look he keeps, this legendary thief is far from storybook charming. Still, his band the Merry Men is wicked-cool.

⇥ ACTIVITIES ⇤
Lead Singer of the Merry Men

⇥ ROYALLY ANNOYING HABIT ⇤
Breaking out into punk rock no matter where he is.

"Buy my demo on the MirrorNet! It's totally Outlaw."

Sparrow plots with Duchess to ruin the True Hearts Day Dance. But even he's getting the feeling that Duchess has ruffled one too many feathers for good company.

Gus Crumb

We've never seen these two sweet-tooth cousins without a handful of sugary treats from the Old Witch's Candy-Cottage store in Book End—and they're quite happy about that! They'll do anything Headmaster Grimm tells them to. But we were able to bewitch a few answers out of them . . . for the right amount of candy.

⊰——ACTIVITIES——⊱

Anything Headmaster Grimm thinks
is important

ONLY

⊰——S~~ECRET~~ HEART'S DESIRE——⊱

CANDY!

Coach Gingerbreadman has to give these greedy cousins detention daily for trying to eat his office.

Helga Crumb

Gus and Helga are technically first cousins, but they behave like identical twins. They act all sweet and innocent (especially if you have sweets to offer them.) Yet somehow everyone at school knows there's trouble brewing when they come around. Perhaps it's the sticky trail of candy wrappers they leave behind wherever they go.

❖—Known For—❖
Finishing one another's sentences

❖—Royally Annoying Habit—❖
Treating themselves to other people's assignments in Cooking Class-ic

"Vhat is dis, my cousin, Helga? Someone has lost their caramels, yes?"

"Perhaps ve should keep them safe, my cousin, Gus—in our bellies!"

Fabelous Faculty

Whether they are former kings and queens, dragon trainers, or potion brewers, the teachers at Ever After High are some of the most legendary instructors in their fields. As Headmaster Grimm likes to say, "Trust in the former storybook heroes and villains to keep you on track toward destiny. They've been there before!" His words ring true. What prince hasn't asked Dr. King Charming for wooing advice? And who hasn't stopped by Counselor Mother Goose's office to let off some teapot steam? From their legends to ours, these are the teachers that keep the storybook destinies burning bright.

Ever After High Headmaster

Milton Grimm

⇜ Relatives ⇝
Giles Grimm, brother

⇜ Education ⇝
PhD in Storybook Legends

⇜ Quote ⇝
"Embrace your destiny!"

Master Librarian

Giles Grimm

⇜ Currently ⇝
Cursed by a Babble Spell

⇜ Office ⇝
The Vault of Lost Tales

⇜ Quote ⇝
"Two tools, one for weeds, one for woods, none with ease. A day is not destined, a lock needs no keys."

Baba Yaga

❖ TEACHES ❖
Spells, Hexes, and General Witchery

FAVORITE METHOD OF DISCIPLINE ❖
Shooting people with her squirt bottle

❖ OFFICE ❖
A thatch-roofed cottage that walks
on chicken legs

GENERAL VILLAINY

Mr. Badwolf

❖ TEACHES ❖
Home Evilnomics

❖ FAMOUS FOR ❖
Family heritage of terrorizing little
pigs and grandmothers

❖ PET PEEVE ❖
Students who chew gum.
It gets stuck in his fur.

Ugh! - his quizzes were the worst!
- Blondie

MUSE-IC

Professor Pied Piper

⁂ TEACHES ⁂
Muse-ic

⁂ EDUCATION ⁂
Majored in Magic Flute;
Minored in Pest Control

⁂ CAN BE FOUND ⁂
Ridding his classroom of rats

SCIENCE & SORCERY

Professor Rumpelstiltskin

⁂ ALSO TEACHES ⁂
Chemythstry

⁂ AFTER SCHOOL CLUB ⁂
Gold Spinning Practice

⁂ KNOWN FOR ⁂
Making students earn hextra credit by
spinning straw into gold

GRIMMNASTICS

Coach Gingerbreadman

❖—COACHES—❖
Track and Field

❖—AWARDS—❖
He holds the fairytale kingdom
record in running

❖—REPUTATION—❖
Although he appears sweet,
he's one tough cookie

TALL-TALE STUDIES

Professor Jack B. Nimble

❖—ALSO TEACHES—❖
Environmental Magic

❖—AWARDS—❖
Holds the school record for the
beanstalk jump

❖—KNOWN FOR—❖
Quirky hat collection

TOO CHARMING FOR MIRRORPHOTO!

PRINCESSOLOGY 101

Her Majesty, the White Queen

⊰ **ALSO TEACHES** ⊱
Crownculus

⊰ **KNOWN FOR** ⊱
Asking her students to imagine six impossible things before class starts

⊰ **FORMERLY TAUGHT AT** ⊱
Wonderland High

HERO TRAINING

Dr. King Charming

⊰ **ALSO TEACHES** ⊱
Dragon Slaying; Advanced Wooing

⊰ **AFTER SCHOOL ACTIVITY** ⊱
Oversees the Dragon-Slaying Squad

⊰ **EDUCATION** ⊱
PhD in Charming

Professor Momma Bear

⊰— KNOWN FOR —⊱

Cooking porridge just right for
the Castleteria breakfast

⊰— QUOTE —⊱

"A good, hot breakfast will give you
energy to follow your destiny!"

BEAST TRAINING & CARE

Professor Poppa Bear

⊰— EDUCATION —⊱

Accredited by the International
Union of Magical Animal Trainers

⊰— PET PEEVE —⊱

Students who sit in his chair.
Or eat his porridge.

MOST DESTINED TO . . .

You voted, we posted! Here are your choices, submitted via the MirrorNet, for this year's "Most Destined To . . ." winners.

Most Destined to
Live Happily Ever After

*Apple White
and Daring Charming,
of course!*

Raven Queen

Class-ic Clown

Madeline Hatter

Most Muse-ical

YOU KNOW IT!
Sparrow

Sparrow Hood

MOST DESTINED TO . . .

Best Wooer

Hopper Croakington II

Most Destined to Plan a Party in Her Sleep

Briar Beauty

Most Destined to NEVER be a Vegetarian

Cerise Hood

Biggest Gossip

Blondie Lockes

Sneakiest!

Best Smile

Kitty Cheshire

To Our Perfect Little Princess,

We always knew you'd follow your destiny.

But even while staying within

your storyline, you continue to astonish,

amaze, and impress us.

Congratulations, our sweet,

sweet Apple!

Love, Mom and Dad

Raven,
You are my daughter.
Never forget that.
— Dad

Fellow students:
I know what you were all thinking—
"How can I express my adoration and gratitude to the most dashing creature who has ever walked these halls?"
Well, I've gone ahead and done it for you (see how chivalrous I am?).

It's blinding me... — Cerise

Here's to my future and totally royal destiny!

~Daring

To our
darling children:
stay forever
charming!

~Dr. King Charming
and Mom

My cherished
daughter,
Kitty,
never stop
SMILING.

—Mom

WHY is My Maddie like a teapot?

Because she is always **bursting** full of **life** (and tea!)

Mischief and Madness always, my child.   Dad

(Brought to you by the Mad Hatter of Wonderland,
Owner of the Mad Hatter of Wonderland's Hat & Tea Shoppe. Do stop by!)

To my beautiful Briar—always remember that life is a dream! —Love, Mom

To My Snooky Wookums, Hopper

Don't worry, son, you'll always be my little Prince! Kisses! Mom

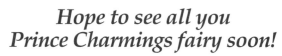

Thanks for all your help planning the True Hearts Day dance! I thought we were totally cursed when Headmaster Grimm caught you carrying those party decorations. Way to save the story with that silly excuse! (Duchess practically lost her feathers, she was so mad!) Have a spellbinding summer! — Cupid

Remember the time we snuck into the Castleteria for a midnight snack? That was off-the-hook! This school really needs better locks. Charm you next year! — Blondie

Thanks for helping me with my Crownculus homework all year. I would have ended up with a major fairy fail if it wasn't for you. Have a spelltacular summer! — Cedar Wood

GIVE 'EM HEX OVER THE SUMMER. YOU KNOW WHAT I MEAN. Sparrow Hood

Now that we have signed, you will give us the candies, yes?

Gus & Helga

I thought the work you did on that Science and Sorcery presentation was pretty cool. Let me know if you ever want to grab a triple-mint mocha at the Hocus Latte.

—Humphrey

Nice job out on the track this year. Those running skills will come in handy when some crazy old baker tries to eat you. Keep it up over the summer.

—Coach Gingerbreadman

It's been a spella-good year. Shoot me a text over the summer. I'm doing the Hex Treme Games again. We'll go beanstalk jumping.

—Briar Beauty

Thanks for making this year enchanting! Be sure to visit me at the Glass Slipper over the summer. I'll let you know when we have the good sales going on!

—Ashlynn